Angel Shoes

For Gwynneth and Megan E.P.

To my Mum and Dad :) S.R.

Text copyright © 2006 Emily Pound
Illustrations copyright © 2006 Sanja Rescek
This edition copyright © 2006 Lion Hudson

The moral rights of the author and illustrator
have been asserted

A Lion Children's Book
an imprint of
Lion Hudson plc
Mayfield House, 256 Banbury Road,
Oxford OX2 7DH, England
www.lionhudson.com
ISBN-13: 978 0 7459 4974 1
ISBN-10: 0 7459 4974 6

First edition 2006
1 3 5 7 9 10 8 6 4 2 0

A catalogue record for this book is available
from the British Library

Typeset in 21/28 Tempus Sans
Printed and bound in China

Angel
Shoes

Emily Pound

Illustrated by
Sanja Rescek

LION
CHILDREN'S

'Come inside!' called Angel's mum. 'Your aunts will be here soon.'

'I wish I weren't called Angel,' said Angel to herself as she stomped indoors from the garden.

'Angels have to do such dull things.'

It seems that angels have to have very clean hands.

They have to wear frilly clothes.

They have to kiss visiting aunts.

And they have to sit indoors listening to grown-ups because going outdoors will spoil their silly angel shoes.

'You've got lots of angel shoes, haven't you?'
said her mother.
'Ooh, we'd love to see them,' said the aunts.

Angel had to show off all her angel shoes.
   There were the shiny shoes with the ankle strap
   and the pink shoes with the button strap;
   and the gold shoes with a tiny bow;
   and silver shoes with glittery ribbons.
   The aunts made ooh noises and aah noises and
mmm noises.

The day after the aunts' visit, Angel's mum had
an idea.
    'I think we should buy you some new shoes for
the summer. Let's go to the shoe shop and get
the kind of shoes that an angel would wear on
a lovely hot day.'

Together they walked to the shop.
'Let's go through the park!' said Angel.
'Not today,' said her mother. 'It's been
raining, and there are lots of puddles there.'
Angel gazed longingly at the swings.

Angel's mum had a lovely time in the shoe shop.
The shop lady brought all kinds of summer shoes.
 Angel's mum liked the pink shoes with bows on.
 They both liked the white shoes with cherries on.
 Then the shop lady found silver shoes with
butterflies on.
 'Those are lovely!' she said. 'Oh, do let's try them
to make sure they fit.'
 They did fit.
 But Angel really wanted
the red boots.

Angel carried the shoes in the shoe bag all the way home. It was nice to have them… but she did wish she could go to the park.

'We'll go tomorrow, if it's dry and sunny,' said Angel's mum.

For going to the park, Angel had to dress in her flower-angel clothes: her flowery top, her flowery trousers, her new butterfly shoes.

As she played, she could feel the other grown-ups pointing and smiling.

She could hear them whispering: 'Doesn't she look like an angel?'

Suddenly, it was all too much.

When her mum wasn't looking, Angel ran off down the wettest path. She could feel the mud squelching round her new shoes.

She jumped in a huge puddle. The brown water splashed all over her. She jumped up and down some more till she was very muddy indeed.

Then Angel stopped to look at herself. She felt a bit alarmed. She had ruined the things her mum liked so much. She wanted to run and hide.

So she ran and ran. It was shady among the trees. The leaves dripped rain all over Angel. She felt cold.

Then she heard a sound: someone was crying.

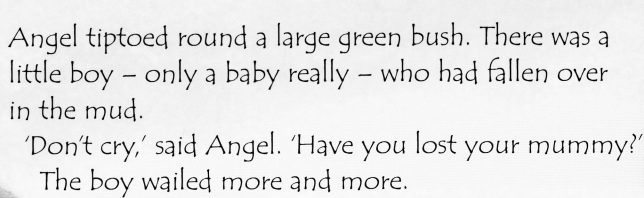

Angel tiptoed round a large green bush. There was a little boy – only a baby really – who had fallen over in the mud.

'Don't cry,' said Angel. 'Have you lost your mummy?' The boy wailed more and more.

'If you follow me, we can go back to the playground,' said Angel. 'We'll find your mum,' Hand in hand, they walked back.

The little boy's mum rushed to hug him.
Angel's mum came running to hug Angel.
'I'm really sorry about the mud,' said Angel.
Somehow, her mum didn't seem to mind.

'Oh, thank you,' said the boy's mum to Angel.
'Thank you, thank you. And you've ruined your
shoes. Oh dear – please, let's go to the shoe shop.
I want to buy you new shoes to say thank you.
Any shoes you want.'

Angel was very pleased with her red boots.

'Now we can go to the park every day, even on rainy days, can't we?' she said.

'I suppose we can,' said her mother.

'Thank you again,' said the boy's mum. 'You're a REAL ANGEL.'

Other titles from Lion Children's Books

Oops!

Pennie Kidd and Rosalind Beardshaw

Does Anybody Love Me?

Gillian Lobel and Rosalind Beardshaw

You Are Very Special

Su Box and Susie Poole